A NORTH-SOUTH PAPERBACK

Critical praise for

Jasmine & Rex

"The familiar-to-adults plot of star-crossed lovers and the complications of forbidden love are romantically presented here for beginning readers, with just enough plot to make for a five chapter book, complete with a rumble and breathless escape. It is Unzner's artwork that gives this book its flashiness, from her sauntering dog-heroes to the saucy flirtatious Jasmine, and on to the fur-flying confrontations between the scrappy animals. Even the requisite last scene of the lovers running away together as the sun rises carries a poignant sweetness that keeps this tale simply delightful."

Children's Book Review Magazine

Wolfram Hänel

Jasmine & Rex

Illustrated by
Christa Unzner

Translated by
Rosemary Lanning

North-South Books
NEW YORK / LONDON

For Hilkje
W.H.

Copyright © 1995 by Nord-Süd Verlag AG, Gossau Zürich, Switzerland
First published in Switzerland under the title *Romeo liebt Julia*
English translation copyright © 1995 by North-South Books Inc.

First published in the United States, Great Britain, Canada,
Australia, and New Zealand in 1995 by North-South Books,
an imprint of Nord-Süd Verlag AG, Gossau Zürich, Switzerland.
First paperback edition published in 1997.

Library of Congress Cataloging-in-Publication Data
Hänel, Wolfram.
[Romeo liebt Julia. English]
Jasmine & Rex / Wolfram Hänel ; illustrated by Christa Unzner
; translated by Rosemary Lanning.
Summary: In this reworking of the Romeo and Juliet story,
Rex the dog and Jasmine the cat fall in love and try to defy
the feud that is keeping them apart.
[1. Dogs—Fiction. 2. Cats—Fiction. 3. Prejudices—Fiction.]
I. Unzner-Fischer, Christa. ill. II. Lanning, Rosemary. III. Title.
PZ7. H1928Jas 1995 [Fic]—dc20 95-15086

A CIP catalogue record for this book is available from The British Library.

ISBN 1-55858-463-3 (trade binding)
1 3 5 7 9 TB 10 8 6 4 2
ISBN 1-55858-777-2 (paperback)
1 3 5 7 9 PB 10 8 6 4 2
Printed in Belgium

For more information about our books, and the authors and artists
who create them, visit our web site: http://www.northsouth.com

Contents

Tiger Trouble

Rover and Rex were the top dogs in town. Whenever the dogs fought the cats, those two good-looking pups would be there, right in the thick of it. And the cats and dogs in this town fought all the time. It seemed as though they'd always been enemies.

But one day something changed. Rex suddenly lost his swagger. Rover didn't know what was wrong with him.

"Cheer up, Rex," he said. "Let's go and have some fun—annoy a few cats maybe."

Rex sighed. "Why are you always looking for trouble?" he asked. "What's the point?" Then he walked away . . .

. . . and straight into trouble! As he
rounded the corner, he came face-to-face
with Tiger. Tiger was big, tough, and
orange as a rusty nail. He was the leader
of the cat gang.

"Got you this time!" hissed Tiger.
"On your own for once."

"I'm with you, Rex!" called Rover,
racing over to help his friend. "Two
against one, easy!"

Then Tiger gave a piercing whistle.
Cats poured through windows and doors,
out of cellars and over walls.

The poor dogs were surrounded. Everywhere they turned, cats leaped at them, snarling and growling.

"Let them have it! Scratch their eyes out!" hissed the cats, slashing with their sharp claws.

"We're done for, my friend," moaned Rover.

"I wanted to end this stupid feud," gasped Rex. "But now I guess it's too late."

The two dogs spun around in circles, growling and snapping. But they were hopelessly outnumbered.

"Every dog has his day, but this isn't ours," said Rover.

All of a sudden it began to rain. Just a few drops at first, then it poured. The cats howled and scattered, running for cover.

"Cowards!" Rover yelled after them. "Scared of a little water! Come on," he said to Rex. "Let's get out of here!"

"Thanks for coming to my rescue," Rex said to his friend. "But I really meant what I said about making peace."

"Maybe someday," said Rover. "But not now. Not after those cats ambushed us, twenty against two. We have to get even. First of all, we'll sneak into the cats' ball tonight, do a little spying."

"It's much too risky!" said Rex, horrified.

"Not if we wear masks," said Rover. "Those tomcats will never recognize us."

At the Cats' Ball

The cats' ball was in full swing when Rex and Rover and their friend Fido arrived.

"Do come in, gentlemen," said the cat at the door, bowing politely.

"You see?" whispered Rover. "These masks fooled them completely."

The ballroom was crowded with cats—cats dancing, cats chattering, eating, and drinking. A band played, a cat crooned into a microphone, and smartly dressed waiters passed trays of food and drink.

Fido grabbed something from a passing tray. "Fish!" he snorted. "Disgusting! Aren't there any bones or dog biscuits?"

"Shhh!" said Rover. "You'll get us thrown out of here, won't he, Rex? Rex?"

But Rex wasn't listening. He was staring across the room as if in a dream.

"Hey," he croaked, clutching at a waiter's sleeve. "Who's the little lady over there? The one with the silky white fur?"

"That's Jasmine," said the waiter. "She came with the big orange cat. I'd stay away from her if you want to keep out of trouble."

"Jasmine," said Rex. "That is the most beautiful name I've ever heard."

He pushed through the crowd, and as he reached her side, he said her name again, with a sigh—"Jasmine."

The pretty white cat turned and looked into his eyes. "Do I know you?" she asked.

"No. My name is Rex. I just had to tell you how beautiful you are."

"Hey, you!" came a growl from behind him. "Stay away from my girl!"

Rex didn't even turn around. He just stood there gazing into Jasmine's eyes.

It was Tiger! He sank his claws into Rex's shoulder. "Did you hear what I said?" he snarled. "Wait, I know you! You're a *dog*! How dare you sneak into our ball! Let me tell you, you won't get out of here alive!"

Tiger raised his paw to his mouth
to give a whistle, but Rex didn't stop to
hear it.

"Hurry, let's get out of here!" he called
to his friends, and the three masked dogs
ran out into the night.

Jasmine's Garden

Rover couldn't get to sleep. Every time he started to drift off, he heard a noise from across the room.

It was Rex. He was wide awake, gazing out at the stars. Every now and then he heaved a loud sigh and thumped his tail on the floor.

"Be quiet over there!" growled Rover. "Go to sleep."

"I can't sleep," said Rex.

"Well then, go for a walk and leave the rest of us in peace," replied Rover.

Rex walked through the dark streets.
No one else was around.

He didn't know where he was going, but
something seemed to draw him on—some
perfume in the air. He followed his nose.

Rex squeezed through iron railings, crawled under bushes, and there, in the moonlight, was Jasmine. She sat high above him on a balcony, gazing at the moon.

Rex watched her, spellbound. He hardly dared breathe.

Then she spoke. "Oh, Rex, Rex," she murmured. "Such a regal name!"

"But . . ." she sighed. "He's a dog, and dogs are our enemies. Can a cat really love a dog?"

"Yes! Yes!" cried Rex, climbing out of the bush. "And a dog can love a cat!"

Startled, Jasmine leaped up onto the
roof. "Who's there?" she whispered.

34

"It's me, Rex," he said, clinging to the gutter.

"What are you doing here?" said Jasmine. "If Tiger finds you, he'll kill you!"

"I'm all right," he said. "The darkness will hide me."

"I'm glad it's dark," she said. "So you cannot see me blushing. You've heard things you were not meant to hear."

"But now I know you love me," he said, "as I love you. I swear by the moon that I love you as much—"

"Do not swear by the moon," Jasmine said quickly. "It changes all the time, and if you love me, it must be forever. But hush! Someone is coming! You must go!"

"Will I see you again?" asked Rex.

"Yes, yes. Meet me in the graveyard at midnight. But hurry now. Be off!" She leaned from the balcony and waved, calling, "Good night, good night, a thousand times good night."

The Fur Flies

"Wake up!" shouted Rover, shaking Fido. "Rex hasn't come back. Come on, we must find him."

"Must we?" mumbled Fido, yawning. Half asleep, he followed Rover outside.

In the street, the last cat was staggering home from the ball.

Suddenly Rover stopped and pointed at a lamppost. "I don't believe it!" he exclaimed.

"What is it?" said Fido, rubbing his eyes.

It was Rex. He was perched on top of the lamppost, a silly smile on his face.

"Oh, boy," muttered Rover. "He's out of his mind."

"Completely nuts," agreed Fido.

"Good *morning*! Good *morning*!" called Rex, grinning from ear to ear. He slid down the lamppost, hopped, skipped, turned a somersault, and walked on his front paws. Then he kissed Rover on the nose.

"What the . . . ?" stuttered Rover.

"Don't say another word," said Rex. "I love her and she loves me. It's as simple as that." And he turned another somersault.

"Who is she?" asked Fido.

"Jasmine, of course. Who else?" said Rex.

"Wha-a-a-at!" gasped Rover. "But she's a *cat*!"

"Yes, a beautiful cat," said Rex. "And I *love* her."

Rover and Fido stared at him, speechless.

"*And I love her,*" said Rex again, even louder.

A man flung open a window and shouted, "Stop that noise!"

"You're waking the whole town," said Rover. Then he groaned. "Oh, no! Look who else you woke!" He pointed at the menacing figure that now stood in front of them, hissing furiously.

"If you want trouble, Tiger, come and get it!" growled Fido, advancing on the big tomcat.

Rex leaped between them. "Please don't fight!" he begged.

"Stay out of this, Rex," warned Rover. "Just because you're in love with a cat doesn't mean they aren't still our enemies." Rover raised his fists.

Rex tried again to stop them. "Why do we have to fight? We could make peace. There's no reason we can't be friends."

"No reason?" yelled Fido. "He's a cat. That's reason enough for me!"

Rex growled. "Then you must fight me first!" He stood in front of Fido.

"You really *are* crazy!" said Fido, turning to stare at Rex.

The moment Fido took his eyes off Tiger, the big cat struck. His sharp claws sank deep into Fido's skin.

Fido tumbled backward. "My eye!" he howled pitifully. "I can't see. I'm blind!"

"No you're not," Tiger taunted him. "You've still got one eye. That's good enough for a stupid mutt like you!"

Rex was furious. He lunged at Tiger, snarling and biting. The fur flew, and blood ran down Tiger's face. His ear was torn. He howled in pain.

"Now you've really done it!" said Rover. "You'd better get away before the rest of the gang turns up. You're a marked dog, Rex. You'll have to get out of town."

"I can't leave. I must see Jasmine. We're meeting in the graveyard at midnight."

"Well, you'd better lie low until then. Hurry, run for it!"

Escape

All was quiet in the graveyard. The gravestones cast huge, ghostly shadows in the moonlight, and the wind rattled the leaves on the trees.

Rex had been waiting there for hours. Lorenzo, the gravedigger's donkey, silently watched him.

A bell rang out from the church tower. Midnight.

Jasmine sprang lightly over the wall.

"Oh, Rex, you're safe," she whispered, her green eyes glowing.

"Not for long," said Rex. "Tiger and his gang are out to get me."

"I know," she said. "He'll never forgive you. He wants to kill you! Even if you manage to survive, there is no way we can ever be together."

"I'd rather die than live without you," said Rex.

"Then we must both die," she moaned. "At least that way, we would be together."

"Don't be stupid," brayed Lorenzo the donkey. "Anything's better than dying."

Lorenzo had been listening to every word, growing more and more exasperated with them. "Run away together," he said. "Go now, while it's still dark."

"But where can we go?" asked Rex. "Tiger is bound to find us!"

"We'll take a ship," said Jasmine. "We'll sail away to a land where it doesn't matter that you are a dog and I am a cat."

"Is there such a place?" asked Rex.

"There must be," said Jasmine.

So they ran away, through the graveyard, along the river, to the bridge, on and on, until at last they saw the sun come up.

"Look! There's the sea!" cried Jasmine.

"And there's a ship!" said Rex. He pointed at a cargo boat, flying flags from all over the world.

The captain was standing at the rail. "Cast off, fore and aft!" he shouted.

"Wait!" called Rex.

"What do you want?" asked the captain.

"We have to get away from here," said Rex.

"Well, I'm sailing away," said the captain. "To the other side of the world. But you can get off wherever you like."

Rex and Jasmine clambered aboard.

"Full steam ahead!" called the captain, and the ship set sail.

Rex and Jasmine stood at the front of the ship, where the wind blew sea spray into their faces. They gazed into the distance and dreamed of the future. They dreamed of a day when the famous feud would finally end, when cats and dogs could live together in peace and harmony, as happily ever after as Rex and Jasmine.

Wolfram Hänel was born in Fulda,
Germany. He trained to teach English and
German, but after working in the theater
he decided not to go into teaching. Instead,
he began to write plays and stories for
children. His previous books for North-South
are *The Extraordinary Adventures of an
Ordinary Hat*, *Lila's Little Dinosaur*, *Mia the
Beach Cat*, and *The Old Man and the Bear*.
He has two homes: one in Hannover,
Germany, and one in Kilnarovanagh, Ireland,
a small village that is also home to a donkey
called Lorenzo.

Christa Unzner was born in a small town near Berlin, in what was then part of East Germany. She wanted to become a ballet dancer, but she ended up studying commercial art and working in an advertising agency. She entered a book illustration contest and won third prize, which led to a career as a free-lance illustrator, primarily of children's books. Her previous books for North-South include *Annie's Dancing Day*, *Loretta and the Little Fairy*, and *Martin and the Pumpkin Ghost*. Christa Unzner lives in Berlin.

NORTH-SOUTH EASY-TO-READ BOOKS

Loretta and the Little Fairy
by Gerda Marie Scheidl, illustrated by Christa Unzner-Fischer

Little Polar Bear and the Brave Little Hare
by Hans de Beer

Where's Molly?
by Uli Waas

The Extraordinary Adventures of an Ordinary Hat
by Wolfram Hänel, illustrated by Christa Unzner-Fischer

Mia the Beach Cat
by Wolfram Hänel, illustrated by Kirsten Höcker

Lila's Little Dinosaur
by Wolfram Hänel, illustrated by Alex de Wolf

Meet the Molesons
by Burny Bos, illustrated by Hans de Beer

More from the Molesons
by Burny Bos, illustrated by Hans de Beer

On the Road with Poppa Whopper
by Marianne Busser and Ron Schröder,
illustrated by Hans de Beer

Spiny
by Jürgen Lassig, illustrated by Uli Waas

Rinaldo, the Sly Fox
by Ursel Scheffler, illustrated by Iskender Gider

The Return of Rinaldo, the Sly Fox
by Ursel Scheffler, illustrated by Iskender Gider

Rinaldo on the Run
by Ursel Scheffler, illustrated by Iskender Gider